D1203079

Willow Rose

LEARNS HONESTY

Willow Rose
LEARNS HONESTY

Written by
MARVIA KOROL
and
MEREDITH MAST

Illustrated By Brittany Fahres

ISBN 978-1-7324511-2-4
Library of Congress Control Number: 2018960233

Printed in the United States of America

First Printing: 2018

18 17 16 15 14   5 4 3 2 1

Illustrations by Brittany Fahres
Cover design by Glen Edelstein
Interior design by Glen Edelstein

SOMETHING

OR **OTHER**

PUBLISHING

Info@SOOPLLC.com

For bulk orders e-mail: Orders@SOOPLLC.com

For Daniel, Andrew, Madeline, Katherine, Nathan, Alexa, Nick, Luke, Patrick, and Joshua, my amazing grandchildren. And to my daughter, Meredith, without whose help, creativity, and inspiration this book would never have had a reason to exist.

Let us read and let us dance—two amusements that will never do any harm to the world.

—VOLTAIRE

Willow Rose woke up one morning to discover she had been planted. "I'm in a garden ... A BEAUTIFUL flower garden," she exclaimed.

2

She fluttered her pretty green leaves, and her rosebuds danced.

3

"You're a rosebush, aren't you?" the flowers in the garden asked her, scowling.
"Yes. I am," she answered proudly.
"Well, you better tell the ants, grasshoppers, and bees,"
they said rudely. They were very mean.

4

"If they land on one of your nasty thorns, they'll get hurt."
They frowned and bent their blossoms away from her.

5

Willow folded her leaves tightly. A tear trickled down a petal just as an ant climbed on her stem.

"Hi," Willow Rose said quickly, shaking off the tear.

Then she added, "Umm ... be careful of my thorns."

6

"You have thorns? You're kidding! I'm outta here," the ant replied, scurrying away.

7

Willow looked around sadly at all the other flowers who were chattering in friendship.

$\mathcal{N}$one of them cared to include her.

Just then, a grasshopper hopped nearby.
"Hi," said the grasshopper.

10

He looked around and saw that there weren't any insects nearby.

"You're not a rose, are you?" he asked.

Willow thought for a moment. She really, really wanted a friend.

Hesitantly, she answered, "Nope, not me."

The grasshopper jumped on Willow's stem and screamed.
"OUCH! Oh ... That hurt! You ARE a rose! You lied to me," he cried.
He slowly hobbled to the ground, sobbing and sniffling, his friendly smile gone.

13

14

Willow felt awful, but before she could think about what she had done, a little bumblebee began circling above. It buzzed close and then flew away. It returned, circled around again, and finally flew close to one of Willow's most fragrant rosebuds.

15

"My name is Butter," it said in its tiny voice. What's your name?"
Willow thought for a moment and answered, "Willow Ro ... um ... Willow."
"Willow," repeated Butter. "Hi Willow. Will you be my friend?"
Willow wanted to have a friend—a special friend. She tried to say, "Yes!"
But she couldn't. Instead she lowered her eyes and whispered,
"No, I'm a rose. I hurt things."

18

Butter giggled. She buzzed and swooped and giggled some more. "Mom told me that roses are the most delicious and most wonderful flower. She also said to watch out for the thorns. If you hadn't told me you are rose, I might have torn a wing. With a torn wing, I can't fly."

With a big smile on her face, Butter announced, "You told me the truth. Now you really *are* my special friend!" And that made Willow Rose VERY, VERY happy.

About the Authors

MEREDITH MAST has been performing, studying, and teaching classical ballet for over 40 years. At the age of 17, Meredith was accepted into the Houston Ballet where she danced professionally for 5 years. Upon retiring from the Houston Ballet, she earned a bachelor of arts degree in psychology from the University of Texas at Austin. After graduating, Meredith pursued a career in human resources and began teaching classical ballet on a part-time basis. After moving to Madison with her husband in 1999, and wanting to work specifically with children, she designed a ballet program for ages 3–9 called Storybook Ballet. The program incorporates classical ballet instruction with costumes, props, music, drama, and the magic of children's stories.

After teaching children for 17 years, and having 4 children of her own, Meredith decided to write her own children's stories to incorporate into her ballet school. With the help of her mother, Marvia Korol, she began writing a series of children's books that were creative, concise, and colorful—each focusing on a particular virtue. Three of their 4 books have been successfully "brought to life" at Storybook Ballet, with dancing, costumes, music, and drama—with much to the delight of her students and families! Not only have her students enjoyed dancing the stories curriculum, but they have also walked away from the class having danced and learned about honesty, patience, kindness, or responsibility.

Meredith's passions are teaching children and sharing her love of ballet. She and her mother hope their books will find their way into homes, schools, preschools, community centers, and other dance schools. She is currently working with her youngest son's elementary school and incorporating the books into their Character Education program.

Meredith resides in beautiful North Freedom, Wisconsin, with her husband and 4 boys.

When MARVIA KOROL counts her blessings, the top of her list includes her husband, 3 amazing adult children, 3 wonderful in-law children, 10 grandchildren, and a recently added "granddaughter" married to her oldest grandson. She has lived all over the United States and spent 4 years in Bermuda. She is recently retired from real estate and is currently rehearsing a part for her local community theater. Throughout her 50+ years of marriage, she's written poetry, too many greeting cards to count, and unfinished novels, and has successfully published a humorous newspaper column. Having been a closet writer for many years, she was excited when her daughter Meredith called to ask for help with a series of children's books for Storybook Ballet. Armed with Meredith's inspiration, guidance, and list of virtues-as-themes, Marvia created whimsical but educational rose gardens, fluffy clouds, and lush woodlands. The final version of *Willow Rose* is the result of their many long phone calls, embellishing and slicing and dicing until both authors knew the book would meet the high standards of Storybook Ballet. For Marvia, who currently resides in sunny Florida with her husband, Peter, and their Yorkie, Calli, seeing *Willow Rose* in print is a dream come true.

24

CPSIA information can be obtained
at www.ICGtesting.com
Printed in the USA
BVHW02n0543221018
530620BV00001B/1/P

9 781732 451124